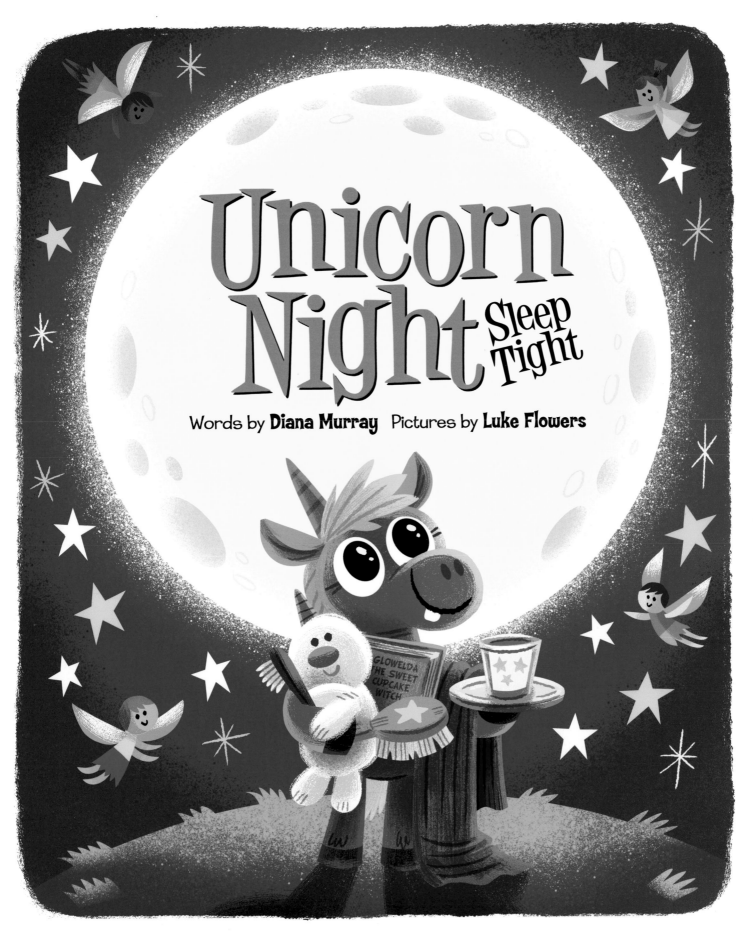

Unicorn Night Sleep Tight

Words by **Diana Murray** Pictures by **Luke Flowers**

sourcebooks
jabberwocky

For Danny, Kat, and Jane.
—DM

For my magi-cool mom and dad. This book is
a celebration of peace, love, and unity. You've
taught me to live, seek, and embrace those
truths throughout my life. A loving
dragon-sized hug to both of you.
—LF

Text © 2021 by Diana Murray · Illustrations © 2021 by Luke Flowers · Cover and internal design © 2021
by Sourcebooks · Sourcebooks and the colophon are registered trademarks of Sourcebooks. All rights
reserved. · The characters and events portrayed in this book are fictitious or are used fictitiously.
Any similarity to real persons, living or dead, is purely coincidental and not intended by the author.
The full color art was sketched and painted in Photoshop using a wide range of unique digital
brushes. · Published by Sourcebooks Jabberwocky, an imprint of Sourcebooks Kids. P.O. Box
4410, Naperville, Illinois 60567-4410 · (630) 961-3900 · sourcebookskids.com · Library
of Congress Cataloging-in-Publication Data is on file with the publisher. · Source
of Production: Wing King Tong Paper Products Co. Ltd., Shenzhen, Guangdong
Province, China · Date of Production: May 2021 · Run Number: 5021666 · Printed
and bound in China. WKT 10 9 8 7 6 5 4 3 2 1

When unicorns
come out to play,
they prance and dance
the day away!

But all that twirling,
skipping, gliding,

cupcake-eating,

rainbow-sliding...

It's exhausting!

There's no doubt.

They get completely
glittered out.

Of course, their parties
are the best,
but unicorns
need time to rest.

They sweep up piles
of dust and sprinkles,
and shine their horns
till each one twinkles.

They brush their manes,
as soft as silk,

and have a sip
of moonbeam milk.

They fluff their pillows—
clouds of white—
and read a book
by fairy light.

Then pull up blankets,
closing eyes,
to sleep beneath
the starry skies.

"Wait a minute."

"Something's wrong!"

"We forgot
to sing the song!"

With voices low,
they snuggle tight
to sing the song
of unicorn night!

Moonlight, starlight, fireflies, fairies humming lullabies...

Woodland creatures
gather 'round,
enchanted by
the soothing sound.

Fuzzy jammies, flower beds,
Sweet dreams swirling in our heads.
Neigh, neigh, neigh, played all day,
time to sleep the night away!

Their singing carries on the breeze.

All who hear it
feel at ease...

and fall into a peaceful, deep,

oh-so-cozy,

dreamy sleep.

They finish singing
with a yawn,
and settle down
to sleep till dawn.

Then all is quiet.

All is right.

Good night, unicorns. Sleep tight.